The Nodders

What! You Don't Want to Nap?

Story by Tina Huggins

Pictures by Brian Schmidt

-Beaver's Pond Press, Saint Paul-

ABOUT THE AUTHOR

Tina Huggins is passionate about teaching, technology, and creativity. She began as an elementary educator and found her love in technology education. She has an MA in Educational Technology and was a national trainer for Apple, Inc. Tina blogs at AppsolutelyYouCan.com and lives in Nashville. For more information, visit www.TheNodders.com.

ABOUT THE ILLUSTRATOR

Brian Schmidt has been lost in the magical world of drawing since he was a kid, creating mazes, castles, and creatures galore. He found his calling as an illustrator after his career in architecture left him wanting more time to be creative. He lives and works in Minnesota's Twin Cities with his wife, Sara. For more information, visit www.BrianSchmidtArtist.com.

ISBN: 978-1-64343-832-0
Library of Congress Cataloging-in-Publication Data

Names: Huggins, Tina, author. | Schmidt, Brian (Brian James), illustrator.
Title: The Nodders : What! You don't want to nap? / story by Tina Huggins ; pictures by Brian Schmidt.
Description: Saint Paul : Beaver's Pond Press, [2021] | Audience: Ages 2-7. | Summary: This whimsical story introduces the Nodders, magical creatures who leave special treats while children snooze. Includes a DIY NapPouch inside dust jacket.
Identifiers: LCCN 2020050729 | ISBN 9781643438320 (hardcover)
Subjects: CYAC: Stories in rhyme. | Naps (Sleep)--Fiction. | Imaginary creatures--Fiction.
Classification: LCC PZ8.3.H86617 Nod 2021 | DDC [E]--dc23
LC record available at https://lccn.loc.gov/2020050729

Printed in Canada
First Printing: 2021
25 24 23 22 21   5 4 3 2 1

Beaver's Pond Press
939 Seventh Street West
Saint Paul, MN 55102
(952) 829-8818
www.BeaversPondPress.com

Edited by Lily Coyle
Illustrated by Brian Schmidt
Production editor: Hanna Kjeldbjerg

To order, visit www.TheNodders.com.
Reseller discounts available.

We've finished our lunch.
Now it's time to take a nap!

Noooo!

Hop into bed with your huggie bear
while I take a seat in my rocking chair.
I'll tell you a story that ends in surprise.
So whatever you do, don't close your eyes!

Imagine an enchanted place, far, far away,
where magical creatures dream and play.

In the Beddy Bye Woods, where it's peaceful and green,
are the loveliest flowers you've ever seen.

There's a sparkling pond as clear as can be
where the colorful goldfish glide lazily.

Near the pond is a giant tree that is older than old,
and it holds a big secret that's never been told.

The many thick branches stretching out far and wide
are covered in knotholes where magic wee ones do hide.

Oh look, see the wee ones with fluttering wings!
Shhhh!
They are Nodders,
and they're very rare things!

They like to play games, like hide-and-go-seek.
They're funny and kind, and what's *really* unique

are their ears—they can hear children miles away.
Their curlicue tuners pick up what you say!

Their jammies' large pockets come in quite handy
for treasures and treats (and maybe some candy).

Their special-made slippers are ideal, heel to toe,
to transport them like magic when they have far to go.

They make fun adventures and love to explore—
Nodders play and they play until they can't play anymore!

As soon as those Nodders start nodding their heads,
they snuggle right into their cozy, small beds.

Sleeping and dreaming are what they do best—
the whole time you're awake, they are having a rest.

In the Beddy Bye Woods, they sleep while you play.
Until YOU take a nap, they can't start their short day!

Because those wee Nodders can hear things so well,
let me whisper this secret that I have to tell:

Awake or asleep, they can hear children shouting.
They also hear laughter, chatting, and pouting.

When "I won't take a nap!" is something you yell,
then those poor little Nodders go under a spell!

They are stuck in their beds,
missing out on their fun.

They can't get up and play if something's not done!

Well,

Old Nonny Nodder planned a plan that is grand
to help children love napping across the whole land.

Announcement

All little children
who get off of their feet
and go down for a nap
get a rare Nodder treat.

If a NapPouch is open
and eyes are shut tight,
that child will wake up
to a tiny delight!

When Nodders hear the first sleepy breath that you take,
they pop out of their beds, wide awake.

They cheerfully rise with a job to do—
they're hoping to give something special to you!

With magic shoes whirling and backpack wings flapping,
a Nodder will peek in to see if you're napping.

Then out of the pocket comes a small treat or treasure
tucked into your NapPouch for your waking pleasure.

Now, close your eyes, little one, sleep nice and sweet,
and when you awake you will find your new treat.

Just turn the knob on your own bedroom door—

to find the treat you are looking for!